NO PLACE
for
FAIRY TALES

edd tello

An imprint of Enslow Publishing

WEST **44** BOOKS™

Cataloging-in-Publication Data

Names: Tello, Edd.
Title: No place for fairy tales / Edd Tello.
Description: New York : West 44, 2023. | Series: West 44 YA verse
Identifiers: ISBN 9781978596320 (pbk.) | ISBN 9781978596313 (library bound) | ISBN 9781978596337 (ebook)
Subjects: LCSH: Children's poetry, American. | Children's poetry, English. | English poetry.
Classification: LCC PS586.3 T445 2023 | DDC 811'.60809282--dc23

First Edition

Published in 2023 by
Enslow Publishing LLC
2544 Clinton Street
Buffalo, New York 14224

Editor: Caitie McAneney
Designer: Tanya Dellaccio

Photo Credits: Cover Ann Muse/Shutterstock.com.

Printed in the United States of America

CPSIA compliance information: Batch #CS23W44: For further information contact Enslow Publishing LLC at 1-800-398-2504.

To Michelle, for daring to be the girl she always wanted to be and sharing her story.

To Caitie, for her commitment and respect; for always being there.

glossary
(in order of appearance)

vecindad: A building containing several housing units.

quinceañera: A celebration of a girl's fifteenth birthday.

ándale: Come on.

pan dulce: Mexican sweet bread.

chambelán: A person (traditionally male) chosen by the girl who is having her quinceañera to be part of her "court."

burradas: Nonsense.

El Otro Lado: "The Other Side;" or the United States.

huevoneando: Lazing around.

peón: Someone who collects municipal garbage in a truck.

chocomilk: A chocolate powder that's used to make chocolate milk.

gordita: A Mexican dish made with masa and stuffed with cheese, meat, or other fillings.

huerco terco: A stubborn kid.

caguama beer: A large bottle of beer, 32 ounces (940ml).

mujer: A woman or wife.

barbacoa: Meat that's cooked over an open fire or slow-roasted.

carnicería: A Mexican butcher shop.

1

fachoso: Ridiculous-looking, wearing a sloppy outfit.

chido: Cool.

tortillero: A tortilla holder or basket.

albañil: A person who lays bricks.

jefecito: A term of endearment for parents.

drogo: A drug addict.

chillón: A constant whiner or complainer.

secundaria: Secondary school in Mexico.

estética: Beauty salon.

carera: Someone who charges a lot for a product or service.

chica: Girl.

pachanga: Party or dance party.

güey: Dude.

padrinos: A couple that sponsors a quinceañera.

cochinita pibil: A slow-roasted pork dish.

Once Upon a Time

there was a girl named Azul
who lived in a poor,
colorful *vecindad*
in Monterrey, Mexico.

Even though Mom calls it
mini-apartments.

This is not
how fairy tales are supposed to start,
but I will be clear:

                         this is not a fairy tale.

In our vecindad,
fairy-tale dreams

         * *shiny tiaras and long gowns* *

usually don't come true.
Not for people like us.

Getting Back to Our Story

Azul was her name.
She felt that name
was the right one.

Not Luis Carlos,
the name her father
called her when he believed
he had a son.

Azul was not a princess yet.
She was more like Cinderella
before the spell.

Helping her mom wash and press,
smelling like laundry detergent.

But Azul was ready
to show our shanty home,
to show the world,
she was not another fairy-tale princess,
but a lifetime queen.

Azul was ready
to have the quinceañera
she imagined in her dreams.
To celebrate the woman she was.

4

I'm Yuriel

and I'm here to help
Azul rewrite her own story
once and for all.

Morning Thoughts

"Hurry up!"
my mom yells
from the patio.

I know the scream
is for me.

Dad's at work
& for months
I've been the only one
within these
peeled walls
in the morning.

Paco, my brother,
left home.
He crossed
the border.

Paco didn't say
anything to me.
He just left a note
inside my sketchbook.

At least
now I sleep
on the bottom bunk
like I always wanted.

On the top bunk,
my sketchbook rests,
but

who am I kidding?

Without Paco's tunes
at full volume
on his phone

& the bathroom door
slamming,

the house has turned into
a deserted land.

I Open the Screen Door and Blink

A dirty chicken jumps
between my feet.

*Whose idea was it to
raise chickens here?*

"Yuriel!
Bring the *Suavitel!*"
Another yell.

I finally react.

I grab the fabric softener
from the plastic bowl
where Mom keeps
the detergents.

"I'm coming. I'm coming,"
I yell back.

*Who does laundry at 8 a.m.
anyway?*

The Dress

"Ándale!
Why you took so long?"
says Mom
without seeing me,
brushing back the lock of hair
that falls over her eyes.

Next to Mom,
my cousin Azul complains,
"Ugh, this dress …
the stain won't come off."

Azul has white hands
from scrubbing so much.

Her arms are strong, like,
twice the size of mine.
Perhaps because
she helps both
her mother and mine.

Her brown skin is
darker than mine,
maybe because
she spends more hours
under the sun.

"Looks like whoever wore that
had a fun night,"
I joke.

Then I start singing
a Jenni Rivera song
about revenge.

Mom nudges me.
"Stop clowning around
and help her."
Azul covers her mouth
and giggles.

"And you stop complaining,"
Mom tells her.

This time I laugh.

Mom sticks clothespins
into her apron and walks over
to the clothesline.

The mad wind
makes Mom's lock of hair
fall over and over again.
But that doesn't stop her.

Suddenly,
shirts and ugly underwear
wave on the clothesline,
dripping with water.

Azul says,
"I just wish this was mine.

If only my shoulders
were less broad …"
She sighs,

still focused on the dress.

Cold Reality

I step into the kitchen.
A damp-rag smell
greets me.

Mom wipes
the plastic tablecloth.

Pan dulce and milk lie there—
a thick skin floats
in the warm white liquid.

It kind of grosses me out,
but I'm so hungry that I dip
the sugared bread in the milk
and swallow fast.

"I wanted to tell you something,"
I say, mouth full.

My mom says,
"Yes, but quickly.
We're not done yet.
The second batch of clothes
is waiting for us."

I say,
"Azul wants
a quinceañera.

With *chambelanes*
and all."

"Uh-huh?"

I nod.

Mom sits and
joins her hands.
"Look, Yuriel."

                    I inhale.

"You know
I'd love to help her,
if that's what you're going
to ask.

I love my *morena*
The same way I love
my sons."

My mom calls Azul
my brown girl
cause her skin is
like brown sugar on
concha bread.

"But right now
isn't the best time for us,"
Mom says.

I exhale.

It never is,
I want to say.
Instead,

I dip
my last piece of bread
into the cup
then take a sip
of the already cold milk.

"Could you at least
ask my brother
to send us some money?"
I ask.

"Ay, Yuriel.
Don't say *burradas.*
Paco
barely found a job.

Do you think people
cross to *El Otro Lado*
and get rich overnight?"

No response.

Mom disappears
out the door.

I Play

with the crumbs
of sweet bread that remain
on the plate.
I press then lick
my fingers.

Before I step
into the morning sun,
I walk to my room.

I grab my sketchbook
and bring it to
the kitchen table.

I try to sketch
a *quince* dress
to give Azul
an idea,

but my howling stomach
distracts me.

I let my head hit
the tablecloth.
Now my face
and my notebook
smell like
an old rag.

My desire
to draw soon

                                   evaporates.

Old Iron

The patio is deserted.

Nobody dares
to be embraced
by the searing heat.

Only Mom,
who washes
our clothes.

There's nothing worse
than having to wash
not only your own clothes but
also other people's.

"Your back must be hurting
by now," I say.

"Just my back? My butt, too.
Especially if my son
spends all day inside
huevoneando."

"Ay, má,
I wasn't lazing around.
I was …
never mind."

My mom ignores me.
"You better bring
that red bucket, *ándale.*"

In the street,
the man who buys old iron
speaks through
the megaphone.
Same old tune.

> *Any old iron you sell.*

And I wish I had
something to sell him.

But

not even my dad,
who works in the back
of a garbage truck
as a *peón,*
brings home
valuable stuff.

> *Drums, refrigerators, stoves,*
> *any old iron,*
> *any old iron.*

I wish I could
sell my sketchbook.

If only it was worth
something …

I wish I could
get some money
for Azul.

The Next Morning, Like Every Morning

since I was 10,
I help Mom
to prepare
lonche for Dad

& his coworkers.
Mom sells them
food for lunch.

6 a.m.

As soon as I hear
the *Ke Buena*
radio station,
I know I have
to get up.

"Come on, Yuriel.
Drink your *chocomilk*
first.

I don't want you
to pass out,"
says Mom.

When I first started helping Mom
with *lonche,*
I looked silly.
Sleepy & inexperienced,
I moved awkwardly
around the kitchen.

Mom sighed
a hundred times.

Little by little,
and after spilling the salsa,
I finally learned.

I started to earn
my first pesos.

Now,

I wrap
the *gorditas* or tacos
in aluminum foil,

carefully put
the salsa
in small bags.
                        Then,

I shower
before walking
to school.

Sometimes

I run out to
deliver the food
to the driver.

Since

my parents
work all day
and Paco's gone,

I'm thankful to my mother
for all I've learned.

Huerco Terco

Saturday morning,
shouts wake me up.

They come from
the house next door.

I put my flip-flops on
and head out
to the kitchen.

I ask Mom,
"Did you hear that?
Where's Dad?"

"He's covering
a shift, and …"

Before she finishes,
I'm already outside.

"Where do you think
you're going?"
says Mom
from behind.

But her words
mingle with dust.

"Ay, cómo eres terco,
huerco!"

Mom always says
how stubborn I am.

I just try

           to be a good son
           to be a good friend
           to be a good cousin

This time,
I need to be the third.

"Stay out of it,
Yuriel!" Mom warns.

But I'm already halfway
to Azul's home.

Yuri

I stare at
the screen door.

My uncle's voice
roars on the other side
as my aunt Conchis cries,
"Luis, stop!"

The thought of
speaking up
makes my heart
skip a beat.

I manage to move
my feet.

A hand grabs me by
the shoulder. It's Mom.
"Come on. Let's go."

Instead, she gives me
the strength I need to stay.

The door opens.

"It had to be you."

My uncle looks
at Mom & me.

Aunt Conchis,
holding plastic hangers
with her plump hands,

looks up at the ceiling,
unable to look
at us.

Perhaps,
she's thanking God
that Mom and I
have come.

"What do you want,
Yuri, huh?"

My uncle knows
how much I hate
being named
like the Mexican singer.

Yuri is a nickname
they gave me
in the neighborhood
when I said I was gay.

He thinks it's funny
to call me Yuri.

"Leave her alone,"
I say,
my voice cracking.

"Mind your own."
His face shows
his disgust.

Azul walks past
her father.
Her teary eyes seek
refuge in mine.

I wonder if
I'll end up
with a black eye.

I wonder if
he can hear
my heartbeat.

"Yuriel, please,"
Mom insists.

But I don't wanna
become my brother's
letdown.
He asked me to
take care of Azul before
he left.

"What, Yuri?
Are you gonna beat me?
Go on!"
my uncle mocks me.

He must see
my fists balled up
& lips trembling.

"Stop it, Luis!
He's just a kid,"
Mom yells at him.

Suddenly, she
makes me feel
so small.

I hold my uncle's gaze and say,

"You're a failure.
As an uncle
and as a father."

Heavy Clothing

"When you finish
delivering those clothes,
you come back here
immediately,"
Mom warns me.

Azul's staring
at the sky.

She has the same gaze
as my aunt Conchis,
dark and deep,
but less drained.
Although
both hide pain.

We walk together,
holding clothes
covered with plastic bags.
The clouds follow us.

Azul finally speaks.
"You know why my dad
acted like that?"

I await her response.

"Because I told him
I want the *quinceañera*.
He said I'll only
make a fool of myself."

I sigh.
"He hit you?"

Azul wipes her face
with the back of her hand.
No tears fall, only sweat.
"No."

"You sure?"

She nods.
"He never laid a hand
on me."

"But you know
what he does to you
is abuse, right?"
I say.

"Keep walking, Yuriel.
I'm tired of carrying
these heavy clothes,"
Azul says.

The Delivery

We arrive at the house.
Similar in size
to my own.

Built of brick, unpainted—
the patio floor
just stones.

Our own clothes are wet
from sweat.
I keep my arms
straight.

I don't want Azul
to judge my smell.
"Put some lemon on,"
she would say.

A shirtless,
semi-bald man,
probably in his 40s,
opens the door.

He walks
a stone path.
He looks at Azul
as if unable
to look away.

Azul flips her hair forward,
uncomfortable.
She gives him the clothes.
"Here you go."

"Come on in,"
he offers Azul.
"I have
the money inside."

His voice sounds
dirty and wrong.

I spy through the door.
Surely his wife
is not at home.

"We'll wait here, sir,"
I say,
my eyes fixed
on him.

I don't want to
get in trouble.

The jerk takes his time.

What if he's dangerous?
What if he has a gun?
He could kill us here.

Again,
the anxiety I felt
before covers me
like a bedspread.

"It's always his wife,"
Azul whispers.

"What?"

"The one
who comes out.
It's never him."

After minutes
that seem like hours,
he crosses the stone path
until he reaches us.

He puts his hand
behind his pants.

My heart drums,
waiting for a weapon,
but it's just
his wallet, stained
with paint.

"Tell your mom
I only had one hundred pesos.
That my wife will pass by
to pay her the rest."

Reluctantly,
Azul grabs the money.

When we get
to the street corner,
Azul sighs and says,
"Guess I'll never get used to it."

"To what?"

I realize how silly
my question was.

Obviously, she means:

*To the teasing
when I walk.
To the looks
when I wear tiny shorts.
To the whistles
when my hips swing.*

To the jerks
and their thoughts.

But she only says,
"To stingy,
lunkhead dudes."

Bad Thirst

Azul and I walk
home.

My parents are
outside.

Mom's sitting on
a plastic chair,
Dad on some
cement blocks.

"Good afternoon."
Azul waves her hand
at Dad.

Dad nods his head.
"Hey."

He looks more serious
than usual.
I don't blame him,
though.

He works from
7 a.m. to 3 p.m.
loading garbage bags
all over the city,

and the heat
hasn't let up.

"Yuriel, get me a
caguama beer from the store,"
he orders.
"I'm thirsty.
Thirst for the bad stuff."

Azul laughs loudly.

Mom rolls her eyes.
"Are you going to
drink again?"

Dad sucks his teeth.
"It's just one beer, *mujer.*
I'm getting dehydrated,"
he jokes.

"Drink some water then,"
Mom replies.

I take
the market mesh bag
from the kitchen.

"You coming with me?"
I ask Azul.

"Ay, no. It's too hot.
I'm going home."

"You'll be okay?"
I ask.

She nods.
"It's just my dad."

Afternoon Shouting

"Come and sit down here.
Have a *caguama*
with your father,"
Dad yells at me
from the patio
as I pour the ice-cold beer
into a glass.

"Let him eat, José Francisco,"
my mom yells at Dad
from the kitchen window.

Mom sets down
a plate with a bolillo bread—
refried beans, queso,
and salsa inside it.

A large Coca-Cola
bottle's sweating
on the table.

"Come on.
I'll bring your father
the beer, Yuriel.
You eat well.
Look at you.
You're skinny
as a rail."

Thorns

Dad is already
on his second *caguama,*
waiting
for the stifling heat
to fade.

I sit on
the plastic chair
where Mom
was sitting.

"How are things
with Azul?"
Dad asks.

"Um, why?"
I ask.

"I heard what happened
this morning."

I roll my eyes.
"You *heard*?
Mom told you,
right?"

He nods
and laughs.

I sigh deeply.
"Azul's alright."

"Want a sip?"
Dad asks.

"Dad, you're not supposed
to invite your own son
to drink."

"Who said that?"

I have no answer.

He takes a long sip
from the glass.
I know something's
bugging him.

Then he starts.

"Do you know
what's been
the craziest thing
about being a
cleaning worker?"

"Um, no," I say.
"I guess
working in the heat?"

Dad shakes his head.
Another long sip.

"When people
put dead plants
that have thorns
in the garbage bags.

Sometimes
they cut through
the working gloves.
Those things are …"

I cut him off.
"Why are you
telling me
all of this?"

"Look, son,
there are some people
who are like thorns.
It is better
to keep them out
of our way.
Your uncle Luis
is one of them."

"Dad, I didn't go to
Azul's for fun.
I went because
she needed me."

Dad's eyes
are already glazed.
"Well, I would prefer
my family
to peel those thorns off.
Do you understand?"

I shrug.

"Yuriel, just stay away
from him."

"You don't
understand," I argue.

Dad scratches
his head.
"You know how
you can help Azul?
By giving her money
for her *quinceañera*.
You need money?"

Of course I do.

"It's not just about
the money, Dad.
And we don't have it
anyway."

I stand up.

My dad just gives me
a look that tells me
he's hurt.

Bloom

It drives me crazy
when the lines come to me
after and not
during an argument.

I would like
to have told Dad,

"I'm not Prince Phillip.
This is not *Sleeping Beauty.*
There are no thorns to cut.
Some flowers just BLOOM
on TOP of them.

Azul is one
of those flowers."

Debts

I walk into the kitchen.

"Yuriel, don't you dare
ask your father
for a single peso,"

Mom says,
sewing a button
on my school shirt.

"Were you listening
this whole time?!"

"Well, your father
was almost screaming."

I breathe out.

Mom says,
"Since Paco left,
your dad has been
very *endrogado.*"
I run a hand through
my short hair.

"Mom, don't bring
my brother into this.
What does he have to do
with Dad being in
deep debt?"

Mom pushes the needle
through my shirt
and says,
"Let me finish this,
or I'm going to prick myself."

Then I think

that Paco owes me
the HIGHEST debt for
outing me with my folks
and leaving me

without any explanation.

Paco Wasn't the First

to notice I was gay.
I think my parents already knew.
Maybe they always did.

But Paco was the first one
to ask me WHY.

He was 10. I was six.

Some school dudes
came up to him:

> *Why does your brother*
> *have a girly voice?*
> *Why does he*
> *hang out only with girls?*
> *Why doesn't he*
> *play soccer with us?*

Paco finally asked me
one day,

Why don't you
act like the other boys?
Why you act
like a freak?

Why, why, why?!
I asked myself as well.

Mom Threw the First Threat

I was 10.

During her
telenovela commercials,
she went to turn
the stove off.

Suddenly,
a shadow from behind
took me by surprise:

Mom caught me
kissing the screen.
Her eyes went from
the cute young actor
        on TV ➔ to me

I froze.

She stepped toward me
with a heavy gaze.
She said,

"Just wait until
 your father gets home."

I didn't eat.
I didn't leave my room.

I didn't feel safe
until the next day when

the school principal called
my parents:
My brother's behavior
problems. AGAIN.

Dad already had
other concerns.
His gay son wasn't
one of them.

Dad Was Next

Two years ago,
our art teacher,
Flor Villanueva,

liked to tell us stories
from all over the world.
Her favorites were
fairy tales.

Later,
we would create something
related to those tales.

Everyone complained
about how childish
that task was.

Not me.
I memorized every detail,
especially imagining
princess seams & crowns.

Ms. Villanueva gave me
white sheets of paper for free.

One day,
Dad saw me lying on
the old, torn-up sofa

while I traced the lines
of a blue dress—
white paper
scattered on the floor.

"Why do you only draw
those dolls?
That's gay stuff."

"They're not dolls,
they …"

                    I stopped.

His sharp look
made me feel
so small.

"Because Yuriel
is gay, pá,"
Paco snapped.
"No big deal, right?"

                The world stopped.

Dad put the toe
of his boot on
my school supplies.

They looked like
the boots of
an enormous giant.

"Is it true, Yuriel?
Is my son gay?"
His face filled
with rage.

The fear
drowned out my voice.

"C'mon. Answer me.
Be a man!" he said.

My falling tears
made him
RAGE.

"Yes, Dad. I *am* gay."

Sunday Doubts

The cackling hen outside
wakes me up
before the sun glares.

The house smells
like freshly ironed clothes.
Mom is wearing
her dress for church.

"Tell your dad not
to buy much *barbacoa*.
I'm not going to lunch,"
Mom says as she opens
the kitchen door.

"Why not?
Are you on a diet now?"
I joke.

She sighs, upset.

"Better hang your towel
on the clothesline. *Ándale.*
Your aunt Conchis
is waiting for me."

"How come?!"
I ask, amazed.

"It feels weird
that she wants
to go to Mass."

Mom steps out.
"Ay, Yuriel.
Who are we
to judge
the Lord's will?"

I roll my eyes.
Then I follow her
to the patio.
"Mom?"

"Now what?"
she asks.

"Why don't you talk
to Father Ernesto
about celebrating
a *Quince* Mass
for Azul?"

"Look, my dear son,"
Mom wipes sweat
from her forehead
with a face towel
and says,

"You know my *morena*
is like a daughter to me,

but for the church,
this religious ceremony
is something …"

"Very judgy?"
I cut her off.
"So now,
who are we to judge,
Mom?"

No Saints

Aunt Conchis is not
a devout Mexican Catholic
who goes to church
on Sundays

even though
she raised Azul & Diana
in that religion.

My mom made me
do First Holy Communion.
Reluctantly, I said yes.
I was just a child.

After that,
she left me alone.

"Better this way.
The church would fall down
because of you,"
she told me when

I refused to confess
to Father Ernesto
about being gay.

Maybe she's right.

The church
would collapse.

It's not like I want
to be a saint,
but I want to support Azul.

Not like Aunt Conchis,
who truly believes that
by going to church,

she will wash away
the guilt of keeping silent
when her husband
mistreats her daughter.

Sunday

We may only have
bread and milk
for breakfast
during the week.

We may be in deep debt,
endrogados, as Mom
constantly recalls.

But on Sundays,
we never miss
barbacoa and
a big Coke.

Dad steps out
of his room, shirtless.

He hands me
a 100-peso bill.

The first thing I notice
is the white sun spots
on his hands.

"Hold the barbacoa tight,"
he says.

"Don't let the stray dogs
take it from you.
Poor dogs are
always hungry."

Before I leave,
he says,
"Your mom's going to the
market after church.

There will be enough barbacoa,
so you can invite Princess Azul
to lunch."

Because for Mom,
Azul is her *morena*,
but for Dad,
Azul is *la princesa*.

It reminds me of how far
my dad has come
in accepting what he cannot change.

Tomás

Azul and I
head for Hidalgo Street.

Azul, wearing red lipstick
and her short hair
gathered in a messy bun.

Me, with my unruly
morning hair and
my distressed T-shirt.

After walking
several blocks,
we finally arrive
at the *carnicería,*
"Los Tres Cochinitos."

Four people wait in line.

A big black speaker
plays banda music.

I can smell the barbacoa
coming from the steaming pot.

My belly rumbles
so hard that I might come home
with an empty bag.

When it's our turn,
my attention shifts from
my stomach to the guy
serving the barbacoa.

He lifts his head.
His hooded eyes
and low-fade hair
make a pit
in my stomach.

It's not hunger
that I feel anymore.

Why is it that when
you are all *fachoso* and basic
you meet hot people?
I hate that.

"So, how much?"
the guy asks.

His tiny earring
catches my eye.

I find myself
biting my nails.
"Huh?!"

Azul giggles
behind me.
I give her a nudge.

"How much barbacoa
do you want?"

I pretend not
to stare at him.
"Sorry. Um,
a kilo is fine, please."

But my eyes fly back
to his thick faded hair
covered with gel.

"Are you new here?"
Azul blurts out.

Wait, why does she——?

He nods as he ties
up the bag and says,

"Yup. My mom
married Toño, so
we moved here.
On Sundays,
I'll help him."

Toño Alvarado
is the owner of the *carnicería*.
Two years ago,
he had an ugly divorce
after he caught his wife
with someone else.
Neighbors gossiped,

64

*Thank God Toño
didn't have his butcher knife
in his room that night.*

Suddenly, I find my hands
holding the bag
with the barbacoa inside.

"Are you from around here?"

The people behind us
look impatient.

"Yeah. We live
a few blocks away,"
I say.

"*Chido.* Guess I'll see you
guys around. I'm Tomás,"
he says.

I move to
the cash register
while Azul
says our names.

Tomás cocks his head,
staring at me.

I'm biting my nails.
Again.

After the Butcher Shop,

we walk to the grocery store
across the street.
"You were gaping, dude!"
Azul exclaims and
opens the refrigerator.

"What are you
talking about?"

She takes out the two-liter coke.
"Yuriel, I'm not stupid.
I know that little face
very well. You obviously
liked that guy."

My stomach sinks again.

"Whatever did you see
in him?" she adds.
"Apart from his greasy T-shirt
and his sweaty cheeks. Ugh."

I only suck my teeth
and shake my head.
"I'll go buy the tortillas,"
I say and walk away.

66

The List

I manage to fit
everything on the table:

small plates with
halved lemons,
cilantro & chopped onion,
and salt.

I get lost looking at
the *tortillero* bopping
from Dad to Azul,
Azul to Dad.
In my mind,
there's only Tomás.

"Maybe you should
make a list," Dad says
through a mouthful of taco.

"A list of what?"
I ask.

Azul rolls her eyes.
"Focus, dude.
We're talking about
the things we need
for the *quince.*"

I sip from my glass.
"So you actually
want the party?"

Azul shrugs and exhales.
"I guess this is the only way
I actually could …"

She clears her throat.
"Look Yuriel,
I don't think I'll have
a wedding dressed
all in white.
At least I deserve
a *quince* dress with
my *chambelanes* knights."

I nod silently.

"Yuriel, bring me that
little notebook your mom
keeps in the drawer,"
Dad says, pointing to
the kitchen cabinet.

"Dad, clean your hands
first!"

"I thought my wife
wasn't here,"
Dad says sarcastically
as I reach for the
notebook.

68

Azul laughs.
"I'll lose the ideas
if I don't write them down,
kiddo," Dad adds.

Azul looks at
Dad's hands and says,
"Hand me the notebook.
I'll write them down."

a dress
the fifteen cake
chambelanes
speakers & microphone
pink disco lights
table arrangements
plastic tables and chairs
tablecloths
food and drinks
father/daughter dance

Azul crosses out
that last thing and
keeps solemnly writing.

"Hey," Dad says.
"I'll dance the waltz
as if you were my daughter.
Don't worry about that."

Respect

After I came out,
you'd think
it was a just a matter of time
before Azul did, too.

It was
way more complicated
than that.

At home,
Mom argued with Dad
about me
every night
while Paco

put on loud music that
drowned out
their words.

Sometimes Paco
would ask Dad outright
to shut up.

Until the glances
that Dad avoided
and the small talk
(Yuriel, how's school going?)
slowly returned.

At Azul's,
a different story
unfolded.

She tried so hard
to avoid any mannerisms
and being caught.

Her father
was an *albañil* and
his fellow workers
always said he whistled
at the trans girls
who worked in a bar
near the construction site.

Azul knew
her dad's feelings
were as hard as a
cement wall.

Since she was tall,
she played basketball
during recess.

What she really wanted:
to win her father's respect,
even if it cost her
tears and sweat.

But last August,
she couldn't take it
anymore.

Rubbing the neck
of her shirt,
she said,

"You know, Yuriel?
One day,
I want to work
as a petroleum engineer.
I have always dreamed
of wearing a Pemex woman's
engineer uniform."

At first, I sneered.
I thought she was
making fun of me
for being queer.

Then she pulled
a serious look.

"Ah, you're not joking,
girl!" I exclaimed.

Azul giggled.

She had earned
not only
my complete trust,
but also my respect.

Not Your Average Cinderella—Part I

Last September,
on the night before
Independence Day,

Azul and I went
to a party at
her best friend Mareli's house.

"I'm fourteen years old, Yuriel,"
she said as we walked.
"I'm tired of pretending."

She nervously
pulled a tube of red lipstick
and a pair of high heels
out of her backpack.

Something I
didn't expect.

Despite the stares
and mockery,
Azul made it to the kitchen
in high heels.

She poured herself
a drink.
Then another.

Pretending to be confident,
cause Azul was just
as nervous as I was,
she moved
to the dance floor.

First,
Mareli joined us.

Then, the other girls
gathered around us
to the sound
of reggaeton.

Azul started to twerk.

Suddenly, a young dude
with a beard and a cap,
around my brother's age,
maybe three years older than us,
looked at her.

She kept dancing.

"Who is he?"
I asked.

She shrugged.

"Just a dude."
Seeing how late it was,
we ran out of Mareli's house,
laughing.

Azul, barefoot,
with her high-heeled shoes
in hand.

We ran through
the dark streets.

Not Your Average Cinderella—Part II

The next morning,
Paco and I woke up
to hollering.
I looked at Paco.
"Hey, Pa—"

"Shhh!"
Paco hushed me.

Then it sounded
like a piece of furniture
being dragged.

More yelling
and name-calling.

"God, why?!
Why you sent me *this*—
as a son?" It was
my uncle Luis's voice.
He used a gay slur
that made my teeth clench.

Paco covered the
San Judas Tadeo tattoo
on his back with a shirt.

"Let's go."
I hopped out of the bunk.
"Wait, did you know—?"

Paco nodded.
"I mean, if I hadn't seen
this dude Abdías
making out with him
after Mareli's party,
I never would
have guessed
he was …"

"She," I clarified.

"What?"

"She identifies herself as …"

Paco snapped his fingers.
"Okay, okay, dude.
Now focus, man.
We don't have time."

"So, are you friends
with that Abdías?"
I asked him.

But Paco was already
running to Azul's.

Not Your Average Cinderella — Part III

My cousin Diana
was standing
outside the front door.

Her thick eyelashes lowered,
looking at her phone.

And her hair, always worn
in a perfect long ponytail,
was loose.

"Where is she?"
Paco blurted out.

Diana's mind was gone.

Perhaps because her raging papi
felt like a stranger.

Perhaps that's why Diana
ended up pregnant soon after.
Only 17.

Paco and I entered
the tiny living room.

"Get out
of my home!"
my uncle yelled at us.

Aunt Conchis cried,
covering her mouth.

"What did you do
to her?" Paco snapped.

I ran to Azul's room.
Sitting on the edge
of her bed
with smudged lipstick,
Azul held her high-heel slippers,
shaking.

"He knows, Yuriel,"
she whispered.
"I made the mistake of
leaving my slippers
in the middle of the room.

Diana asked whose shoes
they were.
Dad immediately knew
they weren't Mom's size."

"Then take *him* out
of my house!"
My uncle's voice echoed
through the door.

"Luis!" Aunt Conchis cried out.
"Stop, please."

"Man, I'm not gonna
tolerate this bull—"
Paco started.

I pushed the door open.

Paco pushed my uncle away.

"We're ready,"
I softly said.

When we stepped out,
Azul rested her head
against my shoulder.

And cried.

My Parents
Sheltered Azul

until September faded.

As Mom cooked,
she would ask Azul,
"School okay?"

Paco gave Azul
his bunk bed.
He slept on the sofa.

"Well, a princess
in the family," Dad stated.

Back to the Present

When Mom gets home,
she scans the kitchen.
Her kitchen.

"Just look at the mess
you guys left."
Her eyes widen.
"You think that's fine?"

Azul smirks.

"You're not going
anywhere until you've
finished washing
all the dishes.

Did you hear me,
Yuriel?"

"Did you hear her?"
Azul says,
covering her mouth.

Mom's still staring at
the kitchen
as she walks away.
I tear the page
out of the notebook
and hand it to Azul.

"Okay, let's get down
to business."

She sighs and
reads the list.

"Sound and light
equipment is the hardest
thing to get," I say.

"Not really," Azul says.
"I've got it covered."

"Um, how?"

She winks at me.
"You done with
the dishes? Need you
to come with me."

"Yuriel," Dad calls
from his room.
"Come get this dirty glass."

Same Guy

"So, where are we going?"
I ask Azul as we walk.

"I told you. To get
the sound equipment."

Rounding a corner,
Azul stops and says,

"It's over there."
She points to a cantina bar.
"But wait. I can't look
like this."

She lets her hair loose
and puts
red lipstick on.

"Are we going to
sneak in?
Azul, we're underage."

"Susi and Mareli
come here
on Thursdays.
You leave it to me."
When we get to
the seedy bar,

a tall, dark-skinned man
sitting in the doorway
stops us.
"Voter ID?"

"A friend is waiting
for me. For us,"
says Azul.

"Voter ID?"
he repeats.

"A-zul?"
A guy asks, surprised.

The same guy I saw
at the after-party
last September.

"What you
doing … here?"
he asks.
The tattoos
all over his body
make him look hot.

But he walks
and talks too slow.
Is he high?

He pats
the security guard
on the back.
"Let them in, man.
They're my friends."

"I can wait here
if you want,"
I tell Azul.

She gives me that
heavy look.
"Yuriel, this is Abdías."

I gulp.

The Note That Paco Left

with many misspellings,
before leaving:

*Yuriel, take care of my jefecitos. They're my
everything. Mom, Dad, and God know I can't stay.
May the Virgin protect you bro cuz now I won't be
able to do it.
Be careful of the freaking drogos. There's a dude
named Abdias. Be careful with him too.
And take care of Azul. I know I messed up with you,
but you know I love you both.
And don't go all chillón.
Be strong.*

As I Follow Azul and Abdías

into the bar,

I wonder,
is this the same guy
Paco talked about?

I just wish I'd had
more time to share
these little things
with Paco.

There's Something about Abdías

I just don't trust.

The way
he winks at Azul or
glances down
at her butt.

Something
I don't like at all.

I have been
staring at Abdías,
trying to figure out
if this guy is *the* guy …

"No-way this is
Pa-co's bro?!"
He lets out
a scornful laugh
and nudges me.

"Dude, your bro-ther
and I were friends!"

Were? Okay.
This is that Abdías.

"Actually,
You want a drink?
I'm eighteen already,
dude, so
I can order one for you."

I shake my head.
"I'm good."

Azul asks him,
"So, will you
give them to me?

"The what?" he says
with a dirty look.

"The speakers and
the mics, you fool."

"What will I
get in return?"
Abdías spanks her,
and she half-smiles.

There's something about Abdías
that makes me feel
uncomfortable.

Unapproved

Monday morning,
Azul and I arrive
at 6:40 at *la secundaria.*

Our high school,
Rodolfo Treviño,
is at the end of
a poorly paved road.

The old redbrick
building is secured
by a yellow iron fence,

but I don't think
anyone here
really feels safe.

Mareli passes through
the entrance
wearing painted nails &
a skirt a bit too short.

Deans don't say
anything to her even
though both things
aren't allowed at school.

Mareli,
releasing her hair,
says,
"What's up, babies?"

Azul snickers.
"How can you
enter like that?"

Mareli shrugs.
"Told the dean
it's my mom's fault
for hemming the skirt
by herself.
She's a salon owner,
not a seamstress."

I shake my head,
laughing.

The bell chimes.

Azul stands,
thinking.
Then says,

"It's kinda unfair.

That time I wore
colorful bangles,
they took them from me.

I never got them back."

A Collection

Mareli and I go in
the same class group, 3A.
Azul is in 3B.

As the students arrive,
Mareli asks,
"What was it you
wanted to tell me?"

"Well, since your mom
works in a beauty salon,"
Azul starts.
"We wanted to see if she
could do my hair and makeup
for my quinceañera."

"Baby, don't even ask!
Of course,"
Mareli squeals.
"I'm so excited for …"

"There's something else,"
I confess.

"Uh-huh.
What's going on?"
Mareli's voice
changes.

I bring
my arms together.
"Thing is,
we don't have
the dress either."

"Wait,
you're planning
a *quince* party,
and
you don't have
the dress yet?!"

Mareli stares
at us in disbelief.

"And we were
wondering if you …"

She cuts me off.
"If I what?
Can I get you
the dress?
Baby, no.
I'm not
a charity."

My shoulders drop.

"Mareli, come on.
We'll be in your debt,"
I say.

"Look,
what we can do
is a WhatsApp group,"
Mareli suggests.

"We could add
our classmates,
Mom's clients,
neighbors,

and raise money
for the *quince* party.
Two pesos, five pesos.
Everything counts."

Teacher Héctor
shows up and
walks into 3B.

Azul groans.
"Ugh. I don't know
if I hate him or
his class more."

We laugh,
and Azul slips off
to her classroom.

Same Blood

Ironically,
the reason why Mr. Héctor
hates me is

the same reason
Ms. Villanueva
used to like me.

Teacher Héctor
is a man in his 50s.
Ill-humored
most of the time.

It seems like he's always
smelling crap,
Dad says.

"Yuriel, if I catch you
drawing again
during my class,

you'll have to
take yourself and
your sketchbook
outside.
Understand?"

In his bald head,
he's always right.
Always ahead.

I call him
"Mr. Creativity Killer."

A Few Weeks Ago

when I went out
to recess,

I glanced at Azul
wearing a school skirt.
Kids were laughing while
the teacher was behind her.

I looked at her
with a "what the heck
is going on" face.

She ignored me
and kept walking
down the hall.

They stopped
in front of the door
of the school
counselor's office.

"Hey!" I let out.
"What happened?"

Azul just shook
her head.
"It's okay, Yuriel."

Teacher Héctor
turned around
and said to me,

"What happened?
Well, it happened
that your cousin Luis

is wearing skirts
and disturbing
the classroom's peace."

I said,
"First, what peace?
There's no peace
without justice,

and this is
clearly unfair …"
My voice grew loud.

Azul's eyes
widened.
"Yuriel, leave it."

"… and second,
her name is Azul.
Not Luis."

"You two," he paused,
"have to be of
the same blood."

"What's wrong
with that?"
I exclaimed.

"You really want
to talk, huh?
Well, you'll also
be suspended
for two days.

And I want
your mom here
tomorrow as well."

Ironically,
the reason why
Teacher Héctor hated me
is the same reason
Miss Villanueva liked me:

for speaking up freely.

Splitting Up

The bell rings
for second class.

Just by looking at
Azul's face,
I know she's
upset.

"Now what?"
I ask her.

"Freaking Héctor
again," she huffs.

"He took away
my phone.

The girls in class
started texting on the
WhatsApp group.

He caught us and
asked who was
behind all this.

I didn't want them
to get in trouble,

so I said
it was my fault."

I sigh. "Azul, I—"

Mareli says,
"Ay, girl,
but if you already
know how Hector is,
why do you ...?"

"Whose side are you on?"
Azul snaps.

Mareli says,
"Hey, easy.
We'll find a way.
We're in this
together, right?"

"I appreciate
your support, but
sometimes I wonder
if this quinceañera
is just a bad idea."

Azul walks away.

After Class

I wait for Azul
outside her classroom.

She's already left.

Mothers, men on bicycles,
food vendors
in their stalls,

wait outside school for
the students
to come out.

Azul is nowhere
to be found.

A part of me
doesn't want to believe it,
but she might be right:

this quinceañera
might be impossible.

Candy

At sundown,
I lift my head
from the bed.

"Look who
finally came out
of his den,"

Mom says to Dad
as she cleans up
the beans and
puts them in a jar.

"Going to the store,"
I say.
"Want something?"

Dad shakes his head.
"No, thanks."

Mom looks at me
with disapproval.

"You're going to buy
your sweetmeats,
aren't you?

You eat lots of candy
and then have no room
for dinner."

I yawn.

"Mom, I just need a
Rockaleta lollipop
to sweeten
my life and start
working on something."

All the Stores

in my neighborhood
sell Rockaletas.

But I walk to the one next to
Los Tres Cochinitos
hoping to find Tomás.

I snoop through
the glass window.

No sign of him.

The speaker's OFF.

Then I remember that

Tomás told us
he would only help
Mr. Alvarado
on Sundays.

Suspended in Time

To shorten
the way home,
I walk across
a vacant lot.

Sitting on a pile
of rusty iron,
where there were
swings long ago,

Tomás is lighting up
a cigarette.

My heart drums.
I try
to look away.

"Hey, man,
what's up?"
he exclaims.

Okay, too late.

I turn to him.
"Hey! Sorry,
I didn't see you."

I feel
my freckled face
burning up.

I can't stop looking
at his eyebrow scar
& his faded haircut
with bangs,
no gel this time.

"It's okay.
Come sit."
He taps an old tire
next to him.

I obey.

Fifteen

"What are you up to?"
He takes a puff.

I don't know
what sounds
more ridiculous,

I was looking for
a lollipop

or

I was looking for
YOU.

I say,
"Just walking around."

He nods,
thinking.
"You ever smoked?"

"No."

He hands me
the cigarette.

"Well, this is
your chance."

He sounds
so confident and
calm that
I give it a hit.

Immediately,
I start to cough.

He laughs.
"How old are you?"

"Fifteen."
I start
coughing again.

We stare at
nothing while
Tomás smokes.

When he's done,
he drops
the cigarette butt
on the grass.

I crush it
under my shoe.
"Do you know that
can start a fire?"

He throws
his hands
in the air.
"Ooh, sorry, man!"

I crack a smile.

"By the way,
how's your cousin
doing?
Azul, right?"

I sigh.
"Yeah. She's fine.
We are just,
um, worried."

"How so?"
I see some concern
in his eyes.

Maybe it's just
my wishful thinking.

"She's had this dream
of a *quince*
for a long time,
but, you know …"
I look away.
"The money."

"Ahh, always
the money."

After a pause,
he puts his hand
on my shoulder
and I shudder.

Then he says,

"Why don't you
look for *padrinos?*

"Like fairy godmothers?"
I tease.

"Yeah!" he says.
"Cake godmothers,
dress godmothers,
godmothers of this
and that.

That's what people do
in these cases,
right?"

I smile.
"You're smarter
than me."

Tomás stands.
"Nah. It's just that
two years ago,
I was fifteen, too."

He shoots me
a wink.

Sitting Outside My House,

Mom and Azul talk.

"And here he is, all carefree,"
Mom says, upset with me.

"The one who was just
going for a lollipop,"
Azul jokes.

"Sorry, má. I ran into a dude
from school."

"A dude from school ..."
Mom repeats, folding her arms.
"It's getting chilly.
Going to bed.
I have tons of clothes
to deliver
tomorrow."

"Good night, aunt.
And thanks," Azul says.

Now Tell Me
the Truth

Azul says.

"I ran into this guy, Tomás,"
I say.

"What? Tomás from
the butcher shop?"

"Yes, him!"

"You sure you ran
into him randomly?"

"Yeeesss! I was
on my way back and …"

Azul cracks up.
"You stalker—"

"Shhh. Listen up. I think
he has a good point."

Azul falls silent.

"I told him about
the *quince.*

He thinks we should
look for *padrinos.*
Like fairy godmothers."

"Well, it doesn't
sound crazy."

"Right? We just
have to hurry."

"I went to the *estética.*
Mareli showed me
several people's messages.

They are more than
willing to help."

I let out
a little scream.
"Great!"

Daydream

Not gonna lie.

Seeing Tomás
and realizing that
there are people
willing to help,

encourages me.

I lock myself
in my room and open
my sketchbook.

First, I only get
crooked lines.
I draw a line, I erase a line.

I bite my nails.

I unwrap my lollipop.

Focus, Yuriel.
I tell myself.

My fingers trace
lines on the paper,
then shapes.

A dress appears.
Since I know Azul,
I add a sash to the dress
and a shawl
to cover her shoulders.

I picture her twirling
at her party.

What if I'm just
daydreaming?

Tuesday Morning
After School

Azul and I look
for a seamstress
from the neighborhood
that Mom told me about.

"People say
she's *carera*,
but let's see,"
Azul says.

A woman with black,
short hair opens the door.
She stares at Azul.
"How can I help you?"

Azul explains to her
what she needs.

She shakes her head.

"Come on, please,"
Azul says.

"No one is gonna
make you a dress that fast,
and on that budget.

Sorry,
but I can't commit."

The tiny woman
is about to
close the door
when I exclaim,

"Well, how about
we pay you more?"

Enchanted

Minutes later,
We're inside
her small house.

"Let's see, let's see."
She puts
her glasses on
and sees the sketch
of the dress I made.

It intimidates me a bit.

"It's just an idea,"
I say quickly.

Azul nods and says,
"Look, I'm a little plump,
so I want to cover these
wrestler shoulders
somehow."

The seamstress smiles.

"Of course not.
You just have
a voluptuous body
like those of
the actresses of
my youth.

You'll look beautiful.
I could make
some little arrangements
here and there, but
this is really good,
especially the shawl idea.
Fantastic."

She turns to me.
"You should study
to be a designer."

"Thanks."
I smile, proud.

Then I think
this career
doesn't come cheap.

Could I really have a happy ending like that?

The seamstress
takes Azul's measurements
and makes some notes.

Azul stays quiet,
looking at her reflection
in the mirror.

"You okay?"
I ask.

"It seems like Dad
will never understand."

She touches herself
beneath her blouse
and sighs.

"I feel like
my body is under a spell,
and I just want
to break the curse."

Fairy Godmother

Mari, Mareli's mom,
washes a lady's hair.

Cynthia, her employee,
is doing someone else's nails

as we walk into
the beige salon.

Haircut posters
hang on the wall.

Plastic hands with nail art
sit on a desk.

"Chica, what a miracle!"
Mari exclaims.

Azul smiles.

"How long until
the *pachanga?"*

Mareli rolls her eyes.
"Mom, I already told you.
Three weeks."

124

Mareli has the same
hazel-colored eyes
as her mother.
Both have long lashes.

I hope that,
unlike her mom,
Mareli finds a good partner
one day.
If she wants to.

"Have you decided
on your look yet?"

Azul says,
"First, I wanted to ask
how much …"

Mari shakes her head.
"Nothing, chica.
Mareli already told me."

Azul beams.
"Well, thanks.
I had some ideas,
but I didn't bring
my phone."

"It's okay.
Look, you have
short hair
for a *quince*.

Would you like
some extensions?"
Mari holds Azul's hair.

"Sounds great!"
Azul gushes.
"And about the makeup …
I'm smooth-skinned,
so don't need shaving.
It's just the acne
on my forehead
from the terrible sweat."

"Chica,
don't even worry.
I'll cover it up.
You'll look fantastic,
you'll see."

"The fairy godmother
also needs a makeover,"
Cynthia looks at me
through the mirror.

I let out a laugh.
I guess that's me.
"I'm fine."

"You just sit back
and relax," Mareli says.

You Look Gorgeous,

Azul says,
tousling my wavy hair.

"Pretty, baby boy,"
Mareli adds.

I cover my mouth
and laugh.
"Stop bugging me,
both of you."

Actually, I kinda like
the haircut.

Cynthia did a French crop
with a slight fade.
An improved version of
the haircut I already had.

"We should stop by
the butcher shop,"
Mareli jokes.
"Let that boy see
how cute you are."

I feel myself blush.
"His name is Tomás.
And no, thanks."

"Hey!" A familiar
voice from across
the street
makes me turn.

It's him.
It's Tomás.

And
he's getting closer.
I feel my face
grow hot.

"Oops. That won't be
necessary anymore,"
Azul says to Mareli.

I wave my hand
clumsily.

Azul and Mareli
burst out laughing.

Get Together

"How's everything
going?" Tomás asks.

Azul can't stop
laughing.

Tomás scowls.
"What? Do I look
like a clown?"

As Azul calms down,
Mareli grins and says,
"Nice earring."

Azul finally speaks,
"Thanks for the
fairy godmother idea."

His gaze falls on me.
"Is everything ready?"

"Almost, yeah,"
I tell him.
"Actually, we're
on our way
to rehearse the waltz."

"What about the dress?
How is it?"
he asks, clearly curious.

Azul's tone is flat.
"It's very poofy.
Turquoise blue."

Tomás eyes' narrow.
"You don't sound
that excited."

"I am!" Azul says.
"It's just I have
so many things
on my mind."

"That makes sense,"
Tomás says.

"You know
what's best?" Azul says.
"That Yuriel
designed it."

That makes
my face blush even more.

Tomás smiles
and says
something,
but I only see
his lips move.

His eyes sparkle.

The next thing
I hear is Azul saying,

"We're having
a casual get-together
tomorrow night.
Just some friends.
Come if you want."

Mareli glances over,
curious to see
my reaction.
They're setting me up!
I put on a poker face.

"I'm not a fan
of *secundaria* parties,"
Tomás scoffs.
"But maybe I'll make
an exception."
He winks at me.
"Yuriel, are you
on WhatsApp?"

And then yes.
I get this goofy smile
on my face.

Tommyland

We walk into
the dance studio.

I'm the main *chambelán*
in the entrance waltz.
Mareli just came
to watch us dance.

All the other *chambelánes*
are classmates.

We start moving
around Azul.
I try to memorize
the choreography.

And it's not that
I have two left feet,

it's just
that I keep thinking
about Tomás's deep voice
and honey eyes.

I lose myself in Tommyland.

Fantasize

The next day
plastic chairs and a table
are set in
the vecindad patio.

Aunt Conchis peeks
through her door.

"I already told you,
only until twelve, eh!"
She warns Azul.
"Your dad will wake up
early tomorrow."

Azul nods.

It's the first time my aunt agrees
with Azul's plans.
I'm impressed.

Azul scans the place.
"We're missing a speaker.
You should ask Tomás
for it." She pokes me.

"The speaker is
from his work. I don't think
he'd lend it to us."

"You know what I think?"
Azul asks as
she wipes down the table.
"That asking for your
WhatsApp number
was just an excuse."

I bite my nails.
"For what?"

She gives me
a mischievous look.
"I don't ask Abdías
for something, unless …"

I laugh.
She's clearly joking.

While cleaning the chairs,
my aunt suddenly says,

"Stop fantasizing
and sweep the place up.
There's dog poop
right there."

Mareli Arrives with Snacks

Doritos and Takis
plus a Bluetooth speaker.

"It belongs to Mom, so
take care of it, babies."

I squeeze her into a hug.
"You're our hero."

Soon, classmates arrive
with beer cans,
cigarettes, and a bottle of
cheap tamarind vodka.

At eight, we're already
a crowd.
Reggaeton plays
in the background.

People talk and dance.
No one seems to care
if the patio smells weird.

At least,
no one complains.

Mareli and I
take Insta selfies with
her new phone.

Azul and some other girls
ball up together.

When I see Abdías
fixing drinks for people,
especially girls,
I remember
my brother's note.

Mareli refills
her Styrofoam cup.

"You're not wasted
yet, right?" I ask her.

Singing a
Danny Ocean song,
she says no.

"Don't take anything
from that güey,"
I whisper.

"Easy, baby.
Let's dance."

We join the gang.
Someone hands me a cup.

When I turn around,
Abdías is smiling.
"Let's get a drink,
dude," he says to me.

"I'm good, thanks."

"Oh, don't be a *sissy*,"
he insists.

"He said no!"
Mareli
pushes him away.

People stare.

"That's why you don't
flirt with anyone, loser,"
Abdías says.
"Without Paco,
you're nothing."
Abdías spits
on the floor.

I want to slap him,
             break into tears.
                       I want many things.

Azul notices and says,
"Everything okay?"
Abdías raises his glass.
"Cheers to Azul!"

137

"Cheers to Azul!"
People shout.

I look toward the street,
wishing Tomás were here.

I grab a tequila shot
and drink.

Drunk People
Tell the Truth

"Luis Carlos!"
my uncle barks
from the kitchen.

Azul is wasted,
so I follow her.

Uncle Luis snaps
his fingers.

"End this now or
I'll call the police
to get all these drunks
out of here."

"No. I won't," Azul says.
"Mom said twelve
and it's …"

"I don't give a—"

"Okay, guys.
The party is over,"
Mareli yells.
"Let's go."

People boo.

"Aside from being born
a girly freak, you came out drunk,"
my uncle mumbles
to Azul.
"What a shame."

"What did you say?"
I ask him.
"Repeat it, jerk."

Those tequila shots …

Mareli claps my shoulder.
"Yuriel, leave it."

I'm about to go
after him when Azul flips
her hair and says,

"You know, Dad?
Maybe that's why
God punished you

by giving you
someone like me.
For being
so homophobic."

Some people cheer,
others clap.

I second that.

Azul is no damsel in distress.

Company

Almost everyone has left.
Only two couples make out
at the patio entrance.

Snack bags and beer cans
litter the floor.

"You and I could go
somewhere else,"
Abdías loud-whispers in
Azul's ear.

It's clear he doesn't want
Mareli and I to hear,
but he's almost yelling.

Mareli holds up some cups.
"You okay, baby?"
she asks Azul.

"Better than ever,"
Azul winks.

But I'm not so sure.

Mareli disconnects
the Bluetooth from her phone
and grabs her speaker.

She sighs heavily.
"I'm leaving.
My mom's outside."

I give her a hug.
"Thanks."

"Azul, you'll stay
with me," I say, firmly.

"Yuriel, Yuriel,
go to bed," Azul sings.

Abdías shakes his head
and smirks.

*Be careful with
him*, Paco had said.

"I won't leave you here," I insist.

Azul rolls her eyes.
Abdías says,
"Man, c'mon."

"Azul, listen to me,"
I say.
"You have two options.
Either come with me
or I'll wake up my parents
and tell them
what's going on."

She exhales.
"Ay, Yuriel, why do you
have to make everything
so dramatic?"

Minutes later,
and after Azul has a make-out session
with Abdías,
Azul and I get home.

The dogs barking outside
keep me awake.

Tomás,
why didn't you come?

I Wake Up to Loud Noises

Slamming doors
& howls of anger.

I look down and notice
Azul's not in the bunk
where I left her.

Groaning,
I step out of my room.

The kitchen light bulb
is OFF.
My parents still sleep.

Nobody
can defend me this time.

Even with
my head foggy
and pounding,
I walk to Azul's house.

Gone

I creep into
the living room.

"For the third time,
it wasn't me,"
my uncle Luis exclaims,
waving his hands.

"I didn't take
that money!"

Azul and my uncle
ignore me
when they see me
standing there.

"Who else, Dad,
if not you?
You were the only one
who opposed
my quinceañera.

The only one
who made me feel
ashamed of
who I am."
Azul runs her hand over
her eyes.

"This community has come together
for *me*—
everyone but you."

Aunt Conchis
reaches over
and grabs my arm.
"Yuriel,
now is not
a good time."

I breathe heavily.
"Azul, you okay?"

"Yuriel, please go,"
Azul whispers,
still sobbing.
"Please,
just go away."

My uncle says
nothing.
He just sighs.

"I just wanna know
what's going on."

Azul walks
to her room
and turns to
her dad.

"Nothing has ever
been given to me, Dad.
And now you're
taking away
my one chance to be happy."

Her tears
don't seem to stop.

"Don't you see?
I just wanted to be
another daughter
to you,
just like Diana is."

Her words
make my heart ache.

She slams the door shut.

Then I go over
to my uncle.
"What did you do?"
I shout.
But he's zoned out.

Aunt Conchis softly says,
"Ay, mi'jo,
don't make things harder.
Go home.
Forget the party
and everything."

"But …"
My voice trails off.

For the first time,
I see the pain through
my uncle's glare.

A pain that I had never
stopped to notice.

Possibilities

I stand in the kitchen.
My aunt has no choice
but to invite me to sit.

She holds
a mug of coffee
out to me.

"Do you have
chocomilk?"
I ask.

She shakes her head
and keeps the mug
for herself.

"Someone stole her money
for the *quince*,"
she mutters as she blows
her nose with toilet paper.

My eyes widen.
"What?"

"Azul thinks it was Luis,
but Yuriel,
I know my husband.

He can be
many things,
but he's not a thief.

I tell her it was someone
from the party,
but she insists that
last night
was just friends."

I try to reason with her.
"Well, if my uncle
wasn't all those other things,
it would be a lot easier
for Azul to trust him,
don't you think?"

She opens her mouth
as if to say something.
Instead, she takes a sip
and then says,

"The math teacher
sent for me
because of the
phone thing.

It was the first time
I stopped at school.
And I noticed
the injustice that
Azul deals with there.

There and everywhere.
It took me a while
to realize
that Azul is …"

I take my aunt's
ridged hands.
Bleached from doing
other peoples' laundry
her whole life.
She cries silent tears.

"It's not easy, Yuriel.
But she's my daughter
and I respect her.

And if she wants
to wear a dress,
she has my support.

And if she wants to
start her hormone therapy,
she has my support.

Because love for
your children is stronger
than anything.
That's how I see it."

I nod.
"Aunty, I think I do
want that coffee."

She smiles.

The way
I see things,
the quinceañera
might not be
a possibility,

but at least
Azul's wildest dreams
ARE.

The Call

I hear Mom sobbing
in her room.
The first thing
that comes to mind is

maybe my aunt
called her to tell her
about the money.

Like in a telenovela
I once watched,
I press my cheek
against the wall.

"Hello, Paco?"
her voice breaks.

"Ask him why
he hasn't called,"
Dad whispers.

"Ay, my son.
We miss you so much.
But, you okay?"
Mom asks.

Then, silence.

"What did you say?
Speak louder, *mi'jo.*"

More silence.

"Ah, okay.
Call us when you can.
Your dad says hello and …"

The phone cuts off.

I stand in front of them.

Mom rests against
my dad's chest.
She turns to me.
"Yuriel …"

I'm biting
my bottom lip.
My hands,
shaking.

Robin Hood

I try to swallow my tears,
but it seems impossible
to stop them.

"Yuriel, we need to talk"
is never a good sign,
even though
I know it's best to listen
to Dad.

I sit next to Mom.

Dad sighs and says,
"I need you to know
about Paco. Why he left.
He messed up
with the wrong people,
son."

I sit straight.

"He … he tried to steal
money from that bar.
The one where
Abdías works.
Abdías promised him
a lot of cash.

One night,
they opened
the cash register,

but didn't know
the owners were
bad people.

Those people
caught them
and beat them up.
It could have
been worse."

Mom looks
straight ahead.

"Abdías ratted him out.
He said it was
your brother who
came up with the idea.

They threatened Paco.
They told him that
if he didn't leave here,
they were going to
kill him …"

Mom's eyes fill
with tears again.

"… and his family."

Why didn't he tell me?
Why did he try to steal
that money—
for his family?
To act like
Robin Hood?
Does Azul know
who Abdías really is?

I have
a lot of questions
that I don't know if
I want the answers to.

I just squeeze my mom
into my arms
and softly say,
"I'm sorry."

Dad shuts his eyes.
Then, tears.

Some Space

On Monday,
Azul doesn't come
to school.

Where is she?
Is she safe?

I don't call her.
Maybe she needs
some space.

I text Tomás instead:

Hey!
What's going on?

I haven't heard
from him since
the day we ran into
him on the street.

When I leave school,
I check my phone.
Zero notifications.

Worried Sick

I walk to
the bus stop.
I take the route
that leaves me
near Lomas del Sur,

where Mom works
for Mrs. Esther Castro,
a nice
rich lady.

The house is
the kind of home
I'd like to have
one day.

The stone exterior
intimidates me,
so I don't ring
the bell.

Mom comes out.
"What now?
What you doing here?"

I run into her arms
and sink into them.
"Mom, I can't.

My brother, Azul …
It's all too much."

Tomás doesn't even
answer my texts, I think
to myself.

"Everything will be okay,"
Mom shushes.
"Look at
the good side.
You have
your family."

Mom kisses
my sweaty forehead.

"Your dad loves you
and accepts you
and Azul.
When we get home,
I'll make you some
valerian tea,
and we'll both look
for Azul."

I cry even more.

My bright side
is Mom.

Decisions

At night, I swing
by Azul's place.

My aunt
opens the door.
"She's in her room.
Just knock first."

The door's open.

Azul seems off.
I plop down
next to her.

"It was him, Yuriel.
Abdías was the one
who stole my money."

My cheeks flame.
I knew it.

Azul breathes faster.

"Do you remember
there was a couple
outside?
They saw him
running down the street."

"But how did
he take it?
I mean, where was
the money?" I ask.

She looks down,
ashamed.
"It was inside
my jeans."

I sigh. "Azul!"

"I was such a fool.
I'm sorry."
Azul sobs.
"I rolled up
the bills and put them
in my back pocket
in case we needed
some money."

I reach for her hand.
"Hey, it's okay.
What should we do?"

She takes
a deep breath.
"We can't do anything.
He's involved
with dangerous people."

"Wait, did you know
him? That he was …"

She nods.

I stand and
head for the door.

"Yuriel, listen
to me. Abdías
promised me
that he would change."

I shake my head.
"Some people
never change.
They're like thorns.
You have to remove them
from the rose."

You Sure About This?

Azul asks me
for the tenth time.

"We can't go around
pretending nothing
happened," I say.

"What if
no one shows up?"
Azul's eyes are
full of worry.
"Or worse yet, if
he carries a gun?"

"Just make sure you bring
your pepper spray," I say.

Honestly, I'm not sure
if we'll be okay.

I just know that I
need to make this right.

Hurt

We wait for
Abdías to arrive.

The same man
from last time
is at the bar entrance,
checking
some people's IDs.

Abdías gets out of
his beat-up white car.

My heart thuds.

Azul walks over
to him, confident.
"Can we talk?"

He side-eyes me.
"What's up? I'm late."

"It won't take long."

Abdías mutters something
to the man.
We walk to the
street corner.

"I know it was you,"
Azul blurts.

Abdías squints.
"What are you
talking about?"

"You took
my money,"
she says.

"It was in my pants
before we kissed.
And when I woke up,
it was gone."

Abdías smiles nervously.
"Maybe it was
your homophobic father,
right?"

"Stop lying," Azul says.
"I'm not here to ask
for my money back."

Knights in Shining Armor

Suddenly,
three guys
get out of a car.

We, Azul's chambelanes,
have always been
by her side.
We are her knights.
Tonight
is no exception.

Abdías looks around.
"What the—?"

We shine
our phone lights
right into his eyes.
Abdías leers.

Azul says,
"I came to ask you
to leave me alone.
I don't want
anything from you.

You only
gave me HURT."

Azul takes big steps
and hops
into her getaway car.
I close the door,
keep her safe.

"Never look at her again,"
I say. The other *chambelanes*
back me up.

We get in the car.

"Hey, stop!"
Abdías ignores us all
and hits the car window.
Then slowly says,
"Okay … okay.
I took the money.
But it was to rent
better equipment."

Azul's on
the verge of tears,
but she stares
straight ahead.
"Go."

Thursday's Sky
Is Clear Blue

Azul, Mareli, and I
agree we won't
go to school.

After the Abdías thing,
Azul insists on
canceling the *quince.*
We all gather
on Thursday
on the vecindad patio.

Aunt Conchis says,
"The neighbors helped
with the drinks, glasses,
and plates.

It would be rude
to say that there
will be no party."

"Mrs. Castro gave me
money to pay for the rest
of the dress!"
Mom exclaims.

"But one
of the chambelanes
left the group,"
Azul complains.
"His mom grounded him
for taking the car
without permission
last night."

Mareli smirks.
"Baby, I learned
the choreography.
I can be
your chambelán, too."

"Now, you *can't*
say no,"
I tell Azul.

Angels

Early Saturday,
while Mari does
Azul's hair & makeup
on the patio,
we get to work.

Schoolmates
come to the rescue.
They take care
of the decorations.

Colored-paper flowers
hang from a banner
that we borrowed
from school.

The name "Azul"
in blue glitter
sparkles
at the center.

We cover the table
with a white cloth
and place the cake
that Dad bought
with his savings.

Neighbors help
to arrange
the centerpieces,

helium balloons
supplied by
the stationery store.

The patio doesn't look
tacky or cheap.

In the kitchen,
my mom and
Aunt Conchis
gossip while they prepare
the *cochinita pibil*.

The scents of spices
and achiote paste mix.

"Yuriel!"
one of the girls yells
from outside.

"A boy came to
drop off a speaker!"

I step out.

Then I notice:
it's the same black speaker
from the butcher shop.

Tomás.

The Biggest Day

I look out the window
of Azul's room.

Guests begin to arrive.

One of Azul's school friends
acts as DJ.

A Bad Bunny song
comes on full blast
from the patio.

"Are you nervous?"
I ask Azul.

She wears her new hair extensions
in soft beach waves.

Her mom puts
a plastic tiara on her.

"Ay, baby girl,
how beautiful you look."
Aunt Conchis sobs.

Mom adjusts
the back of the
poofy turquoise dress.

Azul starts to sweat.
My hands shake.

Come on. Think positive.
I softly touch
the sparkling dress
while biting my nails.

My design come to life.
And the seamstress's job …
how precise and dazzling.

I think about fashion school.

In this moment, anything seems possible.

"Ready, *mi morena?*"
Mom says.

"Thanks for everything,"
Azul tells us.
"This is the biggest
day of my life."

I See the Light

We, the chambelanes,
walk with Azul to
the floor,
wearing big black
rented suits,

even Mareli with
her hair up.

People applaud.
"I See the Light"
comes ON.

My eyes meet Tomás's
while I dance.
And I don't know
what's brighter:

his silver earring
or his smile.

I beam and
glance over at Diana,
Azul's sister.

I don't want to
forget the dance moves.

Diana's carrying
baby Ivana.
She smiles at me.

Once the song ends,
the audience cheers.

In a blink,
we're leaving
the dance floor.

The DJ invites
Azul's dad
to the floor.

Dad fixes his suit,
ready to dance.

But Then

from the entrance,

my uncle Luis
appears.

People fall silent.
Then, murmurs begin.

"Tu Sangre en mi Cuerpo,"
Your Blood in My Body,
starts to play.

Azul hugs her dad.
A big, sincere hug.

They dance slowly.

My uncle holds her face.
Under the white light,
his hands shake.

"I am sorry,"
I read on his lips.
He bursts into tears.

Then, he whispers
something in Azul's ear.
She beams.

The audience erupts
in shouts of joy.

My face red, covered
in tears.

The Surprise

After Azul performs
her unexpected father-daughter dance,
someone says
close to my ear,

"Hey, how well
you dance!"

Right next to me,
Tomás is wearing
a navy blue suit,
smiling.

I shrug.
"Thanks. I mean,
my reggaeton moves
are about to start."

He lets out a laugh.

"Forgive me
for not coming
the other day.
I helped my stepfather
till late."

He sounds genuine.
He really feels bad.

"It's okay,"
I pull my phone out
and say,
"We still have
several hours to have fun.
Plus the hours
you owe me."

He laughs again.
"I'm glad I came then.
I'm all yours tonight."

My face gets hot.
"Well, I …"

"Yuriel!" Azul yells,
dragging her blue dress.
"Come dance!"

In That Moment

All the stars
All the lights & sounds
All those sweaty faces

suddenly disappear.

On the dance floor,
it's just Tomás & me.

Perhaps, after all,

fairy tales *do* exist
and dreams do
come true
for people like us.

At least for tonight.

WANT TO KEEP READING?

If you liked this book, check out another
book from West 44 Books:

ONLY PIECES
BY EDD TELLO

ISBN: 9781978596016

HOME

It's Saturday.
Seven a.m.

The first rays of sun
sweep through
the broken blinds
of our crummy apartment.

The phone rings.
Amá quickly gets up.

I lie in bed.
My eyes are red.
I didn't sleep well.

I manage to
go to the kitchen.

Amá is crying.
She covers her mouth.

I think it's Grandma
she's talking with.

She cries every time
they speak on the phone.

It's been five years
since Abuela last visited us.
We were living in Texas
back then.

But this time,
Amá's face
doesn't look sad.

She hangs up.

It was your father.
He's coming home.

What?
I ask.
Just to make sure
I heard it right.

He's in Bakersfield, mijo.
We will pick him up.
Hurry.
Put some shoes on.

I puff out my chest
and put some jeans on
that my dad gave me
two birthdays ago.

I take
my writing journal
I left
on the floor last night.

Amá washes her face
and mops the floor
a little bit.
She's ready in 10.

A BETTER LIFE

We haven't seen Apá
since we moved out
last January.

We moved to Arvin
'cause my aunt Rosario
told Amá
she could find
more opportunities
in this part
of the country
           a w a y   f r o m   A p á.

He stayed in Texas
for a construction job.

Since both
Amá and Apá
are undocumented,
EVERYTHING
is harder for them.

They need to use
other people's names
and papers to work,
or get paid cash.
Amá's English
is not very good.

She doesn't
understand English
as well
as I do.

She doesn't
go to school
as I do.

My parents
crossed the border
looking for
a better life.

*We did this
for you,*
Mom always
says.

Truth is,
life is not perfect
here.
At least
not for me.

Apá's job finished
some weeks ago.
He couldn't find
a new project,
so he's coming
home.

We will live
together
at least.

Amá's car starts
making noises.

I hope
we don't get stranded
on the road.
It happened
to us once.

It's only
30 minutes
from Arvin
though.

Amá and I
don't talk at all.

I open my notebook
and write.

"THOUSANDS OF PIECES"

a poem by Edgar Jimenez

Sunday afternoon
in the living room.
I'm five years old.

Dozens of pieces
are jumbled
on the floor.

Todas las piezas
deben encajar,
Apá starts.

I already know
all the pieces
must fit.
I do puzzles
in Kindergarten.

Sunny Sunday
on the front porch.
I'm nine.

People setting up
outside their houses
to talk and grill.

Hundreds of pieces
lined up on
the plastic table.

Apá sits
in front of me.
We begin with
the corner pieces.

One day,
I will buy you
one like this,
I say,

pointing out
a big mansion drawn
on the puzzle box.

One month ago,
I bought a puzzle
of the universe.
It still lies closed
under my bed.

Honestly,
I never was good
at puzzles.
Even when we did
the same ones
over & over again.

What I used to love
is how Apá
watched me grow
through those
thousands of pieces.

CHECK OUT MORE BOOKS AT:
www.west44books.com

An imprint of Enslow Publishing

WEST **44** BOOKS™

About the Author

Edd Tello is a bilingual writer of children's
literature. He's the author of *Only Pieces*. Edd
holds a master's degree in creative writing from
the University of Seville and a business certificate
from the University of Washington. He's currently
a high school teacher in Mexico. When he isn't
reading or writing, you can find him drinking
coffee or making his friends laugh with his
anecdotes and jokes. You can find him online at
eddtello.com and @eddstello on socials.